GALAXIES

KATE RIGGS

Creative Education • Creative Paperbacks

Published by Creative Education and Creative Paperbacks
P.O. Box 227, Mankato, Minnesota 56002
Creative Education and Creative Paperbacks are imprints of The Creative Company
www.thecreativecompany.us

Design and production by Chelsey Luther
Printed in the United States of America

Photographs by Alamy (Stocktrek Images, Inc.), Corbis (R Jay GaBany/Stocktrek Images, Robert Gendler/ Stocktrek Images, Imagemore Co., Ltd., Mark Garlick Words & Pictures Ltd/Science Photo Library, NASA-JPL-digital composite cop/Science Faction, David Nunuk/Science Photo Library, Visuals Unlimited), Defense Video & Imagery Distribution System (NASA/JPL-Caltech), deviantART (AlmightyHighElf), Dreamstime (Oriontrail), Getty Images (Mark Garlick, Science Photo Library), HubbleSite (R. Gendler, HubbleSite, NASA/ESA/CXC/University of Potsdam/JPL-Caltech/STScI, NASA/ESA/L. Frattare [STScI], NASA/ESA/Hubble Heritage Team [STScI/AURA], NASA/ESA/S. Baum and C. O'Dea [RIT]/R. Perley and W. Cotton [NRAO/AUI/NSF]/Hubble Heritage Team [STScI/ AURA], NASA/ESA/S. Beckwith [STScI]/Hubble Heritage Team [STScI/AURA], NASA/ESA/A. Nota [STScI]/ESA, NASA/H. Ford [JHU]/G. Illingworth [UCSC/LO]/M. Clampin [STScI]/G. Hartig [STScI]/ACS Science Team/ESA, NASA/Hubble Heritage Team [STScI/AURA]), NASA (NASA/CXC/SAO/JPL-Caltech/STScI, NASA/ESA/Hubble SM4 ERO Team, NASA/JPL-Caltech/P. N. Appleton [SSC/Caltech], NASA/JPL-Caltech/STScI, NASA/JPL-Caltech/ STScI/CXC/UofA), Shutterstock (Maria Starovoytova), Wikipedia (ESO/WFI)

Library of Congress Cataloging-in-Publication Data
Riggs, Kate.
Galaxies / Kate Riggs.
p. cm. — (Across the universe)
Summary: A young scientist's guide to stellar galaxies, including how they interact with other elements in the universe and emphasizing how questions and observations can lead to discovery. Includes index.
ISBN 978-1-60818-482-8 (hardcover)
ISBN 978-1-62832-082-4 (pbk)
1. Galaxies—Juvenile literature. I. Title.
QB857.3.R54 2015
523.1'12—dc23   2014002083

RI.1.1, 2, 3, 4, 5, 6, 7; RI.2.1, 2, 3, 5, 6, 7, 10; RI.3.1, 3, 5, 7, 8; RF.2.3, 4; RF.3.3

First Edition
9 8 7 6 5 4 3 2 1

Pages 20–21 "Astronomy at Home" activity instructions adapted from Exploratorium Magazine: http://www.exploratorium.edu /exploring/space/activity.html

TABLE OF CONTENTS

Did you know that galaxies are collections of **stars**? Scientists called astronomers study galaxies. They have found that there are three main kinds of galaxies. Each kind is named for its shape: spiral, elliptical, and irregular.

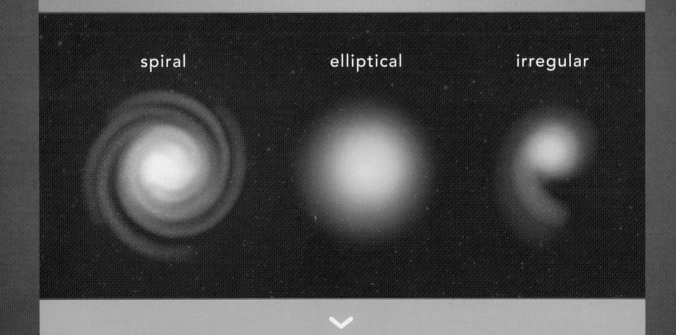

spiral   elliptical   irregular

Our galaxy, the Milky Way, is a barred spiral galaxy.

Andromeda is a neighboring galaxy that can be seen from Earth.

Spiral galaxies have curving "arms." These arms are where stars are made from gas and dust. Elliptical galaxies look like footballs or circles. Irregular galaxies are small and not shaped like much of anything. They make a lot of stars.

Centaurus A Galaxy

Astronomers can see the stars in many galaxies. But they cannot see other things, like black holes. These are areas believed to have so much **gravity** that not even light can escape. Scientists think there could be a black hole in the middle of the Milky Way.

Milky Way

black hole

Black holes might form
when stars die or explode.

In 3 or 4 billion years, the Milky Way and Andromeda may smash into each other.

Italian astronomer Galileo Galilei made a **telescope** to see the stars in the Milky Way.

>

Triangulum is another galaxy close to the Milky Way. It looks like a pinwheel and is a spiral galaxy like ours. Astronomers use space telescopes to look for galaxies. They try to measure how far apart all the galaxies are.

Triangulum Galaxy

pinwheel

American astronomer Edwin Hubble was the first to say that the **universe** was getting bigger.

>

The Local Group is made up of about 30 galaxies. Andromeda, the Milky Way, and Triangulum are the biggest galaxies in the group. Many **dwarf galaxies** are in this group, too. Galaxies are pulled together by gravity. Sometimes gravity pulls so much that galaxies run into each other.

Whirlpool Galaxy, M51 Group

Astronomers can find galaxies that are too far away to see. The centers of distant galaxies are called quasars. They are the brightest things in the universe. Quasars may surround black holes.

A quasar looks bright because of the gas and dust that fall toward it.

Tell someone what you know about galaxies! What else can you discover?

IRREGULAR GALAXIES

ANTENNAE GALAXIES

CARTWHEEL

CENTAURUS A

CIGAR

M106

PERSEUS A

SPIRAL GALAXIES

 **ANDROMEDA**

 **MILKY WAY**

 **NGC 1300**

 **SOMBRERO**

 **SOUTHERN PINWHEEL**

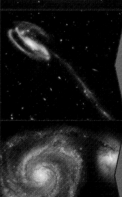 **TADPOLE**

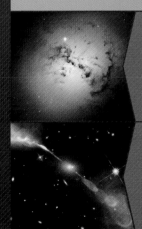 **TRIANGULUM**

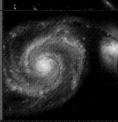 **WHIRLPOOL**

ELLIPTICAL GALAXIES

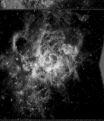 **DUSTY**

ESO 325-G004

HERCULES A

 **SAGITTARIUS DWARF**

MAKE A TELESCOPE

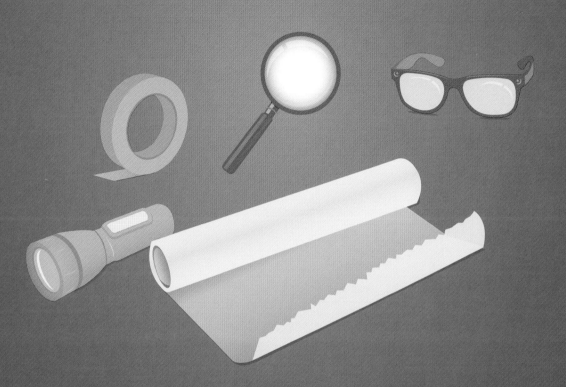

── What you need ──

A pair of reading glasses, a magnifying glass, flashlight, masking tape, waxed paper

What you do

Tape the glasses to a chair back or any upright object. One lens should stick out to the side. Turn on the flashlight and set it on a table far behind the glasses. Hold a sheet of waxed paper for the light to shine on. Walk backwards from the glasses until you see an image of the flashlight on the paper. Then look at the image through your magnifying glass. Take away the paper, and keep looking through your "telescope"!

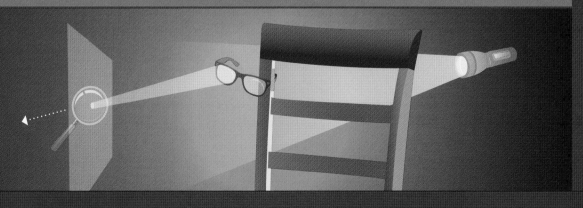

	dwarf galaxies	small systems of several billion stars
	gravity	the force that pulls objects toward each other
	stars	balls of glowing gases located at fixed points in space
	telescope	a viewing tool that makes objects that are far away appear closer
	universe	all the galaxies in outer space

READ MORE

Aguilar, David. *Super Stars: The Biggest, Hottest, Brightest, Most Explosive Stars in the Milky Way.* Washington, D.C.: National Geographic, 2010.

Simon, Seymour. *Stars.* New York: HarperCollins, 2006.

WEBSITES

HubbleSite
http://hubblesite.org/
Look at pictures from space, and learn more about this famous telescope.

NASA's The Space Place
http://spaceplace.nasa.gov/galactic-mobile/en/
Make a galactic mobile with different-shaped galaxies.

Note: Every effort has been made to ensure that the websites listed above are suitable for children, that they have educational value, and that they contain no inappropriate material. However, because of the nature of the Internet, it is impossible to guarantee that these sites will remain active indefinitely or that their contents will not be altered.

INDEX